# When, Then, Will the Devil Care?

## Poems and Short Stories

ROBERT STEPHEN HERRICK

PAGE PUBLISHING
Conneaut Lake, PA

First originally published by Page Publishing 2023

ISBN 979-8-88960-655-0 (pbk)
ISBN 979-8-88960-664-2 (digital)

Printed in the United States of America

For my father, friends and family, my services
and my professors, and any interested readers

# Contents

# The Misplaced Step

The very warm water in the bathroom's tub was a comfort to the injured ex-athlete as he started to soak in its soothing calm for his sprained and bruised left leg. He could hear the winter wind whipping up outside his very small bathroom window, and yet his home was silent inside.

Oddly, a faint sound, like a stick or branch cracking against his garage door or maybe the window to the door, next to it, kept up three or four times. Then a shatter came forth. He had just been recently hit by a drunk driver three days ago, but he didn't have any broken bones from that happening, yet now it wasn't the wind that had his attention or even that accident. He also knew that it would take him over five minutes to safely leave the tub.

A bang from a door being blown open by the wind rattled the man in the tub, and the water sloshed and splashed as he was compelled to jump out of the tub. He banged his left knee on the side of it and bit his tongue to not cry out in pain and anguish as he fell back into the water. He tried to calm down, and when he did, he heard footsteps methodically, slowly stepping up the stairs, one stepping on a creaking step.

The man was nearly paralyzed by pain and fear as the slow stepping approached toward the bathroom door. In mortal terror, the man's mind burned to keep itself together as the doorknob to the bathroom began to turn.

"Who is it? What do you want from me?" the injured man in the tub yelled.

The door slowly began to open, but no one was seen; perhaps they were hiding behind it still. The man in the tub tried again to climb out with stronger resolve but fell again, knocking himself out on the faucet of the tub as it hit his head.

# The Fallen Grace

It was windy and cold tonight, and she parked her car two houses away from her ex-boyfriend's home. She had heard about his accident and thought that now was the time to give him the scare of his life. She became pregnant with his child four months ago, but she called it off due to his verbal abuse. Maybe in his current state of being, she could lay it back on him. She felt that he was going to be in for the surprise of his life.

Upon approaching the house, she picked up a baseball bat—for protection, she felt. She walked up to the side door next to the garage, then felt that she ought to just smash the window on the door to unlock it. The wind was loud, no lights were on outside, and only the small bathroom window was lit. She thought that she was better off taking him by surprise while he was still in the bathroom. Then she swung away.

One thud, two thuds, three thuds, and then a crack. The window to the side door shattered open.

She doubled back for a moment from the strain in her abdomen and the one piece of glass that had cut into her there. Determined and hurt, she unlocked the door and slowly walked into the side room, not closing the door behind her. She started toward the stairs in the living room.

*Bang!* The side door slammed shut from the wind. She jumped and then felt the sting of the cut on her abdomen. She also heard a bang and a splash from upstairs. She looked worried about her pain and checked her cut in the dim light. It was bleeding enough to leave a small bloodstain on her hand and fingers. She was still holding the baseball bat with the other hand.

Maddened by this now, she slowly and methodically walked up the stairs, holding her belly with one hand and holding the bat with the other. A stair creaked, almost causing her to lose her balance. Her mind started to feel torn apart, but she kept her pace and arrived on the second floor.

Down the hallway toward the bathroom, she kept a steady, slow, and methodical pace. She questioned if this was really worth the pain. The pain of his words hurt a lot, and giving birth to his child hurt more, enough to fight through the pain she now had to carry in her body. She got to the door and grasped the knob with a bloody hand and slowly started to turn it.

"Who is it? What do you want from me?" her ex-boyfriend cried out.

She hid behind the door as she opened it slowly. There was a splash and a sickening thud and then another splash. She stopped opening the door and tearfully left the home as quickly as she could. Just the sound of his voice had scared her, as well as that other sound.

With difficulty, she dropped the bat outside and got to her car. She slumped into the driver's seat with tears in her eyes. Her cut felt bigger, and there was a lot of blood on her hand. She drove off slowly, and when she made it home, she collapsed behind the wheel and passed out, bleeding to death.

# The Blackened Circle

See a circle on a wall
And notice a woman with a child on her back
Passing along on her way
Standing tall between steps
Yet with a grimace on her face.

The little child peers out from a papoose
Of cloth and wicker with striped color
Upon the little one's long-sleeved shirt and
A whitish bonnet with mouselike ears
Topping it upon its head
But the child's eyes are worried.

Pressing forward with strain
The woman has her hair pulled into a bun
And is wearing a medium blue kimono,
Yet out behind them there is a whitish backdrop
And the wall in front looks thin in its pattern like
film.

Upon the wall is a blackened circle that looks like
A painted badge with areas slightly
Smeared, subtly yet ominous
It seems to be as the woman with child
Moves on from it standing tall.

Is it to come out of nothing?

Is it to pull out and move on?

Ought it to be simpler and safer?

Should not strength be used to move
Ahead, to stand tall, and to go on?

The blackened circle is a stain
If even walking past it in the rain
Steadily pouring down from dark clouds;
It shuns all numbers but is a holder
For their place
And yet it remains nothing by itself.

# Depths of the Sky

The world lays upon
The rock of the earth
While the depths of the sky
Show fathoms of unknown distance
And can reflect the
Troubles and turmoils
Below.

The crackling of
Lit lighting is
A dynamo breaking
Cracking from its
Reshaping as the
World spreads forth
Further in its
Undertaking.

Thunder rolls from the
Depths of the sky
As trains, Mack Trucks

And vehicles of war
Roll on and on in
Its effigy grinding
Their gears, the sign
Of progressive years
And the weapons of
War explode from
Beneath the atmosphere
Sparking terror.

As a jet plane
Roaring and soaring
Up from the ground
And fireworks bursting
Into the empty air
Collide with the
Space
The race to
Master the awe
And wonderment of
The depths of the
Sky.

The world grows
Larger than life
As the dome above

Remains the same
Never to be
Fully tamed.

# The Ancient Delta's Storm

Calm were the waters now stirred
By a closing element from the air
As the earth and roots take hold
Beneath the raindrops and rustling
With thunder coursing from above.

The air is fresh and alive, leaving
Mist-like conditions upon
The warm, muddy ground which has
A damp, thick, and strong odor
And a saltlike tinge from the sea nearby.

The ancient delta's storm
Has had millennia to come and go
And it comes again in droves
Watering the river's end to the sea
Reviving the surrounding land reliably.

The ancients worshipped these tides
Of moist winds and rolling of up high;
Their deities included the sun and moon
And waters, lakes, and streams, as well as
The animals living in between.

Spirits of greatness arched over the scene
With sparks in the sky crackling down
And the awe of it all was remembered
By story and song reliving it and
Reviving the knowledge of the delta's storm.

# The Faded Red Eyes

One morning, a young boy ten years of age was on his way to school on foot, not by bus. It was his first day in a new school from a new neighborhood. Ricky was his name, and on his way to school, he made what he thought would be a shortcut.

After a few minutes, he lost sight of his path and came upon a shadowed glen. It felt cold. It was rather dark, too. Suddenly, a faded pair of red eyes seemed to peer out at him. Ricky was very scared, so scared that he couldn't scream.

A voice that Ricky could have only heard in his head said to him, "Hello, boy. You seem lost. Do you think that you'll find your way back?"

Ricky's eyes were welling up with tears from fear. He nodded his head, hoping he would be helped by the voice.

The voice was quiet, though the eyes were looking right through the boy, and then it said, "Why did you come here? Are you late for school?"

Ricky's lips were quivering, but he could only make a face without words.

The voice quietly released a grumble, and then it said, "Are you afraid of me? Do you know why?"

Ricky blurted out, "No! I'm sorry!"

The eyes disappeared, and Ricky ran like the wind so far and so fast that he actually was able to find his way back to school. He had nightmares on and off for years. Ricky avoided taking any shortcuts through those woods throughout his school years.

Years later, after Ricky went to college for mechanical engineering, he got into a car accident while trying to avoid a deer. It was dusk, and no other car was involved. Suffering only a mild concussion from bumping his head on the steering wheel, he left his car; and oddly, he went to go looking for the deer into the woods.

Ricky had become a smart man and started to remember the area bit by bit, but dizzy and with a headache, his focus was unclear. However, something in him knew that he was getting close to that spot, and that the deer was also headed in that direction. He shuddered. It was getting cold. It was getting dark, too.

Ricky chose to sit on the forest floor near the dark glen. He felt delirious from the accident.

Suddenly, something prompted him to get up. He couldn't tell why. He started to slowly walk into the glen. Ricky stood there dumbfounded, and then a faded pair of red eyes came into focus.

"Do I remember you? Why are you here? You don't seem well," the male voice said in Ricky's mind. "Can you speak?"

Ricky looked baffled. The voice and the faded red eyes scared most of the wits out of him, but they didn't seem to want to hurt or attack him.

Ricky muttered, "Yes, I think I can speak. I wandered here looking for the deer that I almost hit with my car. I hit a small tree instead, I think."

And then he said, "You don't seem to want to hurt me. Is that true?"

The voice was quiet for a few moments, and then it said, "Young man, you have a lot to learn. I will allow you this. Come further into this glen. The moonlight will show you a gift. Take it and guard it with your life. If you lose it, you will surely die."

Ricky carefully stepped into the dark glen with the faded red eyes seeming to move backward. A glint of something like a jewel seemed to reflect a few moonbeams. Ricky approached it very carefully. His headache and dizziness began to soften.

He said, "Is this it?"

"Yes. Pick it up and put it on your finger. Never come here again," the voice in Ricky's head said. "Leave right now!"

Ricky scrambled to go after putting the ring on without looking back. He kept feeling more clearheaded and somehow knew the quickest path back to his car.

The damage done to his car was minimal, and he could drive away if he chose to. Before driving off, Ricky looked at his finger in the car's light. It was a ring that fitted him perfectly. The ring was tarnished but looked like gold, and it had two red gems fitted side by side.

Ricky was not the same since that evening. He became colder, more reserved, and more critical toward others. However, his keen insight into detail and clearheadedness became a value to his new job, and his promotions came quickly. He never took the ring off, but he also never dated or started a family. Oddly, it didn't seem to bother him. He left town on one of his last promotions to live in a big city out west.

Being successful in his job became his life's work. Everything else could not meet with a priority of the same strength. Ricky finally died of old age when his ring slipped off his bony old finger. He was ninety-eight. One of his business partners did his memorial service and wake for him, as his family had all passed away before him. His ring was buried with him by request on his will, and all his assets went to his latest and last project: a skyscraper.

# The Void

Nothingness…

Emptiness…

Numbness…

To be inside it is
To be unconscious;
Without deed,
The void
Has no need to please
Its captives
For eternity.

Worthlessness…

Speechlessness…

Thoughtlessness…

The void
Is nothingness,
And so are those
Placed within it;
It exists
Without anything
Existing within it
Like a graveyard
For spirits
Wayward from their
Initial path,
And mindlessness
Has put them
Therein.

Silence…

Blackness…

Numbness…

The death of a
Living spirit lies
Within the void,
Frozen as a thing
To be forgotten

By whichever being
Can cause the
Entry to
The void.

# In the Silence

One dark and stormy night,
In the deepest hours of the morn,
A plastic bag
Upon its own initiative…

Had allowed itself to be caught in a breeze,
And it passed across a window's pane;
I was half awake, sitting upon
The cloth-covered couch
In a room lit by dim light from outside,
And the shadows seemed to move
By their own free will.

The night was silent,
Except for the strange breeze outside,
As I struggled to stay awake;
A shadow moved
Like a human quietly walking

From a door but in silence,
And it began to walk into the room
That I was sitting in.

It eerily crept forward slowly;
Then it approached
Around the couch that I had sat upon;
The shadow of a man came
Behind where I was sitting, yet
I could not move or speak from fear
As it stood behind me,
Leaning over me; then I heard
A crash of thunder as
My mind passed into darkness.

I've never had an explanation, though
I've had worries of what else was done
When my mind was enveloped by night;
Such things from a shadow of a man
Upon its own initiative.

# A Piece of My Youth Remembered

I remember back in September of 1984 or 5, when my brothers and I played the eight-track tapes of our dad's favorite seventies rock music; we would go crazy and run all around the house, playing them. That aggravated our mom when she was taking care of our baby sister. She had to yell at us to stop. When our dad came home from work, he would growl and bellow at us to stop if our mom was still busy; and often, we did. But the day of the hurricane, we all had to hide in the basement from its dangerous conditions.

The stockade fence, nearly eight feet high, crashed and was flattened down. The rains flooded over our in-ground pool, and our honeysuckle bushes were buried under the weight of the fence. Not much was said as we listened to the volatile winds ripping off large branches that fell down from the taller trees. The most troubling part for me was the worried crying from my mom and my baby sister during the first part of the storm.

My older brother dared me and my younger brother to go out during the eye of the hurricane, and we did with our dad watching us. It was appalling how much damage and destruction was done. The crashes we had heard were huge branches that had struck down upon our swing set, not just the lightning and thunder. We saw the fence and the pool, and I was feeling exceptionally spooked being out there. But very soon, the winds started to whip up again, and we had to quickly get back to the basement.

Our poor mom was livid that our dad had let us up there outside. When the storm's horrifying sounds came back, the basement itself was eerily quiet. My mom and dad were mad at each other. My brothers and I hoped to be able to hear our dad's music again soon, and we felt the stern quiet was like a punishment harsher than the hurricane itself. Our mom and dad wouldn't even look at each other. Even our little baby sister was rather silent, too.

We never got to hear that enjoyably intense music again that day, and our mom actually told my dad to throw those eight-tracks out. My dad hid his eight-tracks instead, and it took us days to find them. I still remember that September.

# On the Wind

Air surrounds us all
From dry, spacious mists
To tornadoes with wide vortexes;
It travels all around the earth.

With sea and ocean currents,
It brings us weather throughout
All of the world as it carries
The measures it receives.

From calm, cool summer breezes
To icy, sharp winter winds,
It is volatile, unpredictable,
But it is always here or there.

On the wind, things seem to move
When they otherwise couldn't;
It plays on our ears and fears, yet
Without air, we couldn't live or even hear.

Air sustains where earth cannot be,
Air fuels fires and can aid them to spread;
Air brings water vapors to collect them
To form clouds, to bring rain and to pick them back
    up again.

On the wind,
Nothing stays the same;
Change presides with it,
And it seems to play a game.

On the wind,
Anything may come our way
As it flows like rivers
And spreads across the earth in waves.

# Hoping for Dawn to Come

Hoping for dawn to come,
Many may yearn for its light
To warmly wish for some
Comfort and color from
All of its glory and might,
Yet the small bees hum
From flower pistil to the thrum
Of their hives, hoping for the sight
Of their work well done from
The beginning of the dawn to come.
Many may yearn for its light,
Many may still be bees on a mum
As the dew collects colors, as some
Others in homes hear right
The humming hives like a drum
And see the vast beauty come
Forth like the sun with vibrant light,
And as the day is nigh to come,
The bees and the trees live in a pulsing thrum.

# How Love Hurts

The cold darkness outside is cast over with thick snow flurries. Inside, in a forty-two-home apartment complex, a young woman named Cassie is sitting in front of a three-year-old computer monitor, surfing the web. Her boyfriend, with whom she lives, is approaching a ringing telephone.

He picks up the handset and hears, "Hey, how ya doin'?"

"Okay. Cassie and I are going to have supper soon. What's up?"

"Not much right now. Just callin' to see if you have plans soon. So, Andy, you have other plans then?"

A grunt comes over from the seat next to the window of the apartment, right in front of the monitor.

Cassie exclaims, "Just tell him we're having supper when I'm done on here."

"Oh," the voice on the other side of the receiver states, "I see. It seems that your woman is keeping you busy. Well, Annie's my bitch."

"Cassie's my bitch," Andy says.

A roar from the computer area erupts, and as Andy looks over, something very solid strikes him, knocking him down like an anvil.

"What?" explodes Cassie. "What the hell did you say about me?"

She stomps over to Andy, who is lying on the floor, dazed from pain. Cassie keeps blowing out obscenities and kicks the chair right next to his head.

Andy starts to come to and sees his favorite coffee mug about half a foot away from his face on the floor under the kitchen table.

"What the…" Andy deliriously mumbles.

He numbly reaches for the phone and hears from the receiver, "It looks like I caught you at a bad time."

The receiver clicks, then a dial tone.

Cassie, bending down to Andy, hasn't apologized for her excessive use of force, except to calm down from smashing her foot onto Andy's head.

"Do you think I want your friend to think I'm a bitch? Do you?"

Andy's face is still burning, and he is also quite dizzy.

"Will you answer me? Do you think I'm a bitch?" Cassie demands. "Get up, you wuss. Don't disrespect me again."

Andy ignores her but struggles to get up. He's still a bit delirious, but he's somewhat happy for her company as she finally cools down. She makes good slow-cooked soup, he figures.

"So even if you don't deserve my soup, be thankful that I'm letting you have some, jerk," Cassie bitterly states. "Do you like it?"

"Um, yeah, it's good. Thank you."

"You apologize too much for the wrong things. Why do I put up with you? Don't answer that."

Andy keeps working on finishing his soup despite the headache.

"You love me, don't you? Don't call me that again. I'm sorry," Cassie says with some compassion.

Andy is quiet for a moment, then says, "I love you enough to let you stay here, and I'm sorry about what I said on the phone. I didn't realize how bad it was. Thank you for the soup."

He also says through his delirium, "Where's my coffee mug? I'm thirsty."

# Thirteen Ways of Looking at a Coffee Mug

I
A color of
Cobalt-blue covers
Inside and out
Of a coffee mug.

II
Warm tan coffee
Is filling half
Of an unwashed
Coffee mug.

III
A coffee mug
Rests upon the
Corner of an aged wooden
Filing cabinet.

IV
Decorated with thin whitish lines
And an emblem from
A college,
A coffee mug is cherished.

V
A coffee mug holds a mixture
Of cocoa, coffee, and creamer
For a mocha.

VI
Overused and aging,
A coffee mug sticks its
Base to the table.

VII
Pondering its uses,
Instant oatmeal
Can find a way
Out of a coffee mug
With a spoon.

VIII
Tap water and
Sparkling apple grape cider

May meet the bottom
Of a coffee mug.

IX
A coffee mug may
Meet with black coffee
And molasses and be
Held up to let them
Loose and be imbibed.

X
A coffee mug may
Not just be
Only for coffee.

XI
A coffee mug is
A vessel for a
Fair number of things
To travel into the
Thirsting mouth and
Throat of its holder.

XII
Placid is the empty
Coffee mug awaiting

For its vacancy
To be filled.

XIII
A coffee mug bears
Exclusive devotion
And may retain
Traces of its use
As a thin film
Of additional aged coloring.

# A Touch of Time's Hand

Feeling the seconds pass
Moment by moment, one
Can catch the hand of
Time's light grasp and
See it fleeting past.

A touch of time's hand
Is like sensing a
Still breeze as it is
Moving along its path,
Hoping to continue unabashed.

Days and months and years
All pass on by
With memories of the past
And plans for the future
Reflective of the human mind.

A touch of time's hand
Brushes the psyche subtly,
And piece of mind may
Come and go, though
Life continues with its flow.

Live for the present,
As that is where time
Can be seen, but
Strive as you are able
To feel a touch of time's hand.

# A Circumstance of Faith

Faith reminds me of a car accident that involved my ex-wife, myself, and her cousin and how we survived it. I do not view faith as being a consistent thing; however, it is hope with the strength of willpower added to it. Here is a story that may better explain what faith is to me.

One night two-thirds of the way through November in 2002, I was with my new girlfriend. It was about six days after we began dating. Her younger male cousin was with us, and she was driving as I hadn't had my driver's license. We were headed up to Canada to visit with her grandparents and family for Thanksgiving.

I knew that it would be a long trip, and noticing that the fuel gauge was less than half full, I mentioned for her to get gas before we headed up from West Springfield. She seemed unhappy that it was brought up and said that she wanted to refill the gas tank at a place in Newport, Vermont, near the Canadian border. She said that the gas up there was a lot cheaper.

I was worried about this, but she was driving; she wasn't in the mood to get gas before she left.

We left near midnight, and not much had happened during the car ride yet. I was chewing on a French baguette and drinking out of a two-liter bottle of root beer. She was angry at one point, because I accidentally backwashed into the soda bottle.

After an hour or two, my worries softened. Maybe we would be okay. In fact, I had some bizarre feeling that if there were trouble, we would still be okay. Then by two o'clock in the morning, I noticed that the wind was picking up with light snow breezing over the patches of ice on the road. I fell asleep soon after that set of observations, lulled by the radio's tunes.

I woke up to a nightmare. The poor woman that I was with had hit a patch of ice while traveling over forty miles per hour, trying to get to the Canadian border on a near-empty tank of gas. We were passing over another road too.

Being jarred awake and hearing screaming, I reached through the spinning car's force to clasp the passenger-side door handle, hoping that I would not fly into her, and I was braced for impact. Suddenly, the car smacked into the guardrail on my side of the car and whipped me back into my seat. I had crouched down during the spinning and winced on the left side of my face while bracing.

We could have fallen down into the other road below if something hadn't angled the car just right. Something had to have intervened. I thought about this as we ended up in the breakdown lane, facing our original course of direction. The engine had been knocked out of the car, and the firewall had saved our lives.

She frantically asked me if I was okay, and I said that I guessed I was; I muttered it in a muffled tone. Her cousin seemed very quiet, yet usually he was a joker. I was sore, but I could move all my toes, fingers, and limbs fine. I felt a weird tingling, burning pain in the left side of my face, in my left arm, and in my hands, as well as a stiff crick in my neck. What stunned me the most was that we were alive even if the car no longer had an engine.

In my initial thoughts, I did question her judgment about the problem with the gas. The gas tank was on vapors at the time of the accident. I had faith that we would make it up to her grandparents' home okay, trouble or not.

In fact, after two hours or less, at a police kiosk near Newport, Vermont, where we were keeping warm during the wait, her grandfather came by from the other side of the border to pick us up. Her cousin was saying what he could about what had happened. Mostly, I was still a little too tired, stunned, and sore to add much toward the conversation.

Faith can show itself in many ways, even despite potentially fatal circumstances, and I'm more thankful that there weren't any other cars to have been seen at the time of the accident. Even more so, I was thankful for that police officer finding us promptly in that freezing weather, as we were miles from civilization at that spot. Most importantly, we survived the accident, and we were able to walk out of the car without much of a problem. Even if we weren't fully okay, we did get to our destination.

Later that day, we checked back at the accident sight to see the resulting damage in the sunlight. The engine was ripped out of the car, but the bangs and dents were superficial otherwise. Again, we commented on how the firewall had saved our lives. I had faith that we would make it to her grandparents' home, and we did. I wasn't expecting how we did or how sore I would be. But we still got there alive on an element of faith, an empty gas tank, and a very sturdy firewall.

# Ode to the Silhouette of the Moon

Darkened amid
Shadows from clouds
Shadows from the sky,
A moon just new
In the view of its
Silhouette
Slim and crescent-like it
Pales itself in the
Deep reaches of nighttime
And of the fire's light;
So simple and slender
So sleek almost
Serpentine and silvery
That it seems to cut
Into the black sky like
A fileting knife that
Creates severance
From the old

From the past to
Beckon on
To the new
Yes, you
Silhouette of the moon
Beckon out from the
Void of night
From the terror of
The darkened sky
To show, to see
The sliver of hope which
Proves that you
Are neither weak
Nor empty.

# When Again Will I
# See My Little One?

Good health fills the cheeks
Upon my little one's curious face
And her eyes shine brightly.

A pleasant slope for her nose
And baby teeth lost
To her young age are displayed
Upon her smiling face
And her light-brown hair
Highlighted by natural hues
Of paler auburn and russet flow
Down past her rounded shoulders.

Energy abounds around her
Younger limbs as activity
Keeps her heart strong
And her eyes are bedazzled with
Carefree thoughts and dreams

Looking for fun and games and
Anything that may satisfy
Her wide interests.

I see my little one as
A collection of rays of hope;
She has her words come forth with
Excitement and sometimes silliness
And seldom may she show sadness.

A bundle of good things
Like a treasure trove
Is her imagination
And her creative streaks are filled
With diverse interests of revelries
Of her youthful childhood.

Still, she can be cranky
And grumpy and restless
Just like me.

She smiles with youthful mirth
When she gets to see me
And we know that it's often
Not quite enough but
She enjoys our time together

And she leaves a piece of treasure
Upon paper with pencil or marker
Before she needs to go.

She can still smile back at me
Through her grandmother's
Or mother's car window
Though her eyes show sadness
As we know we'll have to
Wait again to share
Our time together.

She has been a beacon of light
For my life and she shows
That she knows it well and good.

My little one grows
More and more each day
With a kinder heart and
An open mind that remembers me
And that does its best
To keep her okay.

# Watching for an Arm of God

"Hi, Adam," a younger woman's voice speaks in a softer tone. "How's the project coming along?"

She has just quietly opened a large steel door to enter a very big, open room. Then she closes it.

"Slow, but I happened to find another piece to the puzzle," he states. "And it has something to do with the sun."

The two of them are in a college observatory in the Midwest. Adam is a young professor of astronomy, and the young woman, Jillian, is one of his prize students. Adam is working on a breakthrough to better explain the activity of the solar system.

Also, he allows Jillian to call him Adam, because for some reason, Professor Slater doesn't sound as welcoming from her. He has also allowed her to help him with this solar system project since the beginning of this semester for extra credit. No other students have taken the initiative to be involved. Most of his students don't take him seriously. Jillian seems to.

"So, Jillian," Professor Adam Slater asks his attractive, prize student, "my current hypothesis on solar activity seems to point on how sunspots and solar flares affect certain regions in the solar system, including the earth.

"Sunspots seem to show a brief dissipation in the sun's rays, and solar flares can spark periods of a global warming effect. If the earth in orbit is close enough in the arc of the flare-ups, the warming from this may happen. Also, Jillian, solar and lunar eclipses can take their own effects."

Jillian has slowly and cautiously been moving closer to Adam while he has been calmly speaking to her, yet his eyes are focused on his notes. She has a hint of awe in her eyes and a bit of something else. Adam doesn't seem to notice.

"You know, Jillian," Professor Adam Slater begins again, "I think that if we focus on the solar flares, we might be able to finish the extra credit assignment. What do you think?"

Jillian is lost in thought. She's imagining curling up on Adam's lap, stroking his dark-auburn hair, feeling his warm breath on her neck with his arms wrapped around her. She scrambles to gather her senses back together.

Throughout the entire semester, she has been doing her best to maintain a 3.741 GPA and takes her studies seriously. However, she has recently begun to study Adam, Professor Adam Slater, a little too seriously. She has just now realized this and stammers.

"Adam, what about that Arm of God hypothesis? It's the one where a solar flare of such magnitude could reach out towards the earth and burn the earth's surface. Does that help?"

Adam turns his head toward her. He sees how close she has gotten, and he widens his mouth into a big grin.

"Wonderful! That fits in the last piece! Now all we have to do is watch for one by looking at the frequency of how many smaller solar flares pop up and gauge for any increase in the sizes. Jillian, I'm filing an A+ for you. Thank you for being so observant."

Jillian softly forces a smaller smile. She is still imagining being close to his long arms, his bright smile, his soothing gray eyes, and his rounded shoulders. She knows that he's very smart, definitely cute, and very enthusiastic. But he's too lost in his work.

She warmly says, "Thank you, Adam. Thank you for making the extra credit available. Maybe I'll see you next semester? I've got to go. I'm sorry, but I don't feel very focused."

"Oh, I'm sorry," the professor calmly states. "I do hope you'll feel better, Jillian. Thank you, too. In my free time, I'll be watching for an Arm of God. Great job."

Jillian slinks off. She pouts and walks off to her car to head home. As she gets to her car, Jillian sighs and frowns from leaving out of embarrassment. Her face tingles and looks a bit darker in hue than her blush shows.

"Why did he let me call him Adam anyway? I hope that he doesn't do that to anyone else," she utters as she steps into her car and drives home, hoping to never let herself fall in love with another professor again.

After all, they're not supposed to date students, she thinks. Maybe after she graduates, he'll be fair game.

At the college, Professor Adam Slater slumps in his chair, murmuring about missing Jillian. He still feels that she is the only person at the college who took him seriously. He reviews her notes and notices a pattern unfolding. There actually is a chance for an Arm of God to happen, and he wants to know when.

# An Arm of God

The intense heat
Of a blazing sun
May reach our homes
With the warm rays
Of its light.

Scientists say
That a solar flare
Can arc out
From the sun's surface
And that we must beware.

An Arm of God
Could reach out
To our homes
And scourge the surface
With unknown purpose.

The surface of
Our planet could melt

And a pandemic
Catastrophe may be
Resulting from fire.

An Arm of God
Is speculative but
Our sun is not
Always as it seems
And cannot be directly
Seen without scientific
Means.

# Ode to a Blank Page

Flat and often
White
Without being
Ruled or lined,
Yet possibilities are
Beyond basic
Comprehension as
Anything goes
Upon your pristine
Paper trimmed to
Any length and width
Inviting creativity
To be
Made manifest by
Any medium chosen
For use;
A blank page open,
Ready to receive
Any color by crayon,
Pen or pencil,

Watercolor, but still
Blank page you capture
It all as much as can fit;
The wonders of the
Universe may be
Shown upon you
As your value
Persists past even
The most tiny of
Marks upon you,
And yes, you, blank page
Will allow and adorn
Both love and scorn
As upon you is filled
Out the mind's plan.

# About the Author

Robert Stephen Herrick is a known local poet in Westfield, Massachusetts. He has archived works at Holyoke Community College with a poem of his on public display for a mural in the Kittredge Building placed there in 2013. He is an alumnus there, as well as of Westfield State University and the University of Massachusetts Amherst. He is an honors student, and he has poems archived at the Westfield Athenaeum and Forum House/Viability in Westfield, Massachusetts.

He hopes that you enjoy his works and find his accomplishments solid and supported.